Weird & Wonderful Tales

Incredible Stories

TONIA THOMAS

PARTRIDGE

Library of Congress Control Number:		2020901564
ISBN:	Softcover	978-1-5437-5623-4
	eBook	978-1-5437-5624-1

Print information available on the last page.

To order additional copies of this book, contact
Toll Free 800 101 2657 (Singapore)
Toll Free 1 800 81 7340 (Malaysia)
orders.singapore@partridgepublishing.com

www.partridgepublishing.com/singapore

Introduction

After college, I realized that there were certain happenings in my life that I never got lessons on at any of the regular schools I attended. There were storms that I went through and questions in my heart that needed urgent answers. Even though I was regular in church, I thought God was a far away phenomenon until He visited me, and spoke with me which marked the beginning of a new life for me. He alone had the answers to my questions.

The happenings around me suddenly stirred me up to the reality of the spirit realm and the need to understand the implications of my mediocrity in that area. Several experiences I have had in life reiterate the existence and nearness of God as well as the spirit realm.

I was not looking for God but He located me and re-directed my life. I learnt that equipments manufactured at some factory come with a manual, which must be strictly adhered to, otherwise spoilage is evident. I realized that God manufactured me and had a manual for my life which He wanted me to know and follow. I discovered how real and close He could be thus an uncommon quest for more of God was born in me which has been exhilarating and satisfying.

This book therefore is a narrative of some unusual happenings I came across and how I navigated through. I believe it will answer some unspoken questions and help to situate some experiences you might have had. This book is thrilling and valuable. Indeed, it is *Weird and Wonderful*

Happy Reading!

Dedication

To God Almighty the Author of Life

Contents

1

Deadly Charms

My phone rang. It was from our headquarters office. They were concluding plans of making me boss as the most senior in the branch office. They were replacing my boss for some misbehavior she did.

I was to be discrete about the takeover while I awaited my letter. A week or two later, rather than get the letter, one of my colleagues showed up to announce to us that he was the new boss as the former had been relieved of her post.

I wondered what had happened back there.

I learnt later that while I was quietly waiting for my letter there was lobbying going on and money was changing hands. Eventually, it went to the highest bidder.

He was my colleague, I gave him his due respect but he was wicked and mean to everyone. He had all the vices you could think off…. girls, money, alcohol….

After a couple of years, his posting suddenly came to another organization while I was to replace him. He didn't like it and was not ready to leave. He decided to ignore directives from headquarters and set up a stooge crony whom he brought from somewhere to replace him. Luck ran out against the two of them and I was installed boss.

The day I was to resume in that office, the Lord warned me not to remove my shoes and not to sit on his chair. I changed the chair and did not remove my shoes. After a couple of weeks, again I heard God's voice that instructed me to change the rug of the office. It was a massive office; the rug was beautiful so why did God want it changed?

I had no access to funds yet, so how was I going to get a new rug. I decided to call a clerk whom I gave instructions to get his team to remove the rug.

To my surprise he told me that some new rugs were kept somewhere and promised to exchange the rugs by the weekend. The following week, a new beautiful rug was laid and I was glad. However, the clerk reported that they found some charms under my table as they changed the rug.

It became suddenly clear to me why God had said I should not remove my shoes.

The weird part of it was that my staff concluded that there was no way the charm could have been physically put under the rug because the big mahogany table under which it was placed had been in that position for more than a decade; it would have taken at least four hefty men to shift it from its position; there was no sign at all that the rug was cut. It was therefore concluded that the charm was commanded spiritually under the rug.

The next question was who could have done it? Was it the boss or the crony that he brought? The answer was not farfetched. The clerk said that on the day the boss was evacuating his personal things from the office, which was his last day in that office; he had sent the clerk to buy three envelopes. He hastened to buy the envelopes because he assumed boss wanted to give them money but he never did. What then was the envelope for? The clerk narrated that the boss had locked himself up in the office shortly before he vacated the office. That was probably the time he was saying his incantations. Also, the three envelopes were a unique color which he recognized immediately he saw them under the rug.

Where did they put the charms? I inquired.

They were in a flower jar by the balcony of the office. I asked them to bring it when suddenly I heard God s voice again warning against it. I therefore told them to burn it. As soon as they set fire on it, my phone rang. Guess who? It was boss. He didn't have time for pleasantries. He rebuked me sternly for not calling him to remove his charms and burning them without his permission. Then he switched off his phone on me.

I was shocked that he had the effrontery to claim ownership of the charms. I wanted to ask him why he would put charms in an office on the last day he was vacating the office. I also wanted to know how he knew that they had set fire on his charms. I wondered how he would have flown an hour or travel twelve hours by road just to come and retrieve his charms, had I told him. Something was obviously amiss.

I saw boss shortly afterwards and was shocked to see that he had emaciated beyond recognition. He died the same year.

2

The Narrow Escape

I was returning from a journey with plenty luggage and had been waiting for a while at a bus stop for a cab to take me home. There were lots of people waiting as well. I eventually found a *keke* (Indian tricycle) driver who after some negotiations was ready to drop me at my location. In my bid to put my luggage in the *keke*, a lady heard probably as the driver told his colleagues his destination and quickly jumped into the *keke* while another boy also did the same. *Keke* can only take three people. The driver asked them to come down from the *keke* and tried to explain to them that I had hired him to take me to a specific location but they refused to come down from the vehicle.

As I put my luggage in the boot of the *keke*, I signaled to the driver to allow them share the *keke* with me and that it would be a bonus to him. Then I turned to the girl and asked her to move in so that I could sit but she told me very rudely that she wanted to sit at the side of the *keke* and not the middle. It was offensive to me and I could have asked her to come down from the *keke* but I didn't argue a bit with her.With the amount I was paying the driver, I was doing her a favor to share the vehicle with me but I conceded to her and sat in the middle.

Barely had we started the journey when an oncoming vehicle faced us and refused to leave our lane. It was obvious something was wrong as I watched our driver trying to veer off the road from the oncoming vehicle. The driver of the coming vehicle was a lady who was learning to drive without an instructor and had panicked as we approached her; she didn't know what to do than to run us over. In a split second I saw the boy on my right jump out of the *keke* before the collision happened. I was thrown to the seat where the boy was.

The *keke* was mangled and the girl was on the ground. People came to our rescue as I managed to come out unhurt from the wreckage. The girl and the driver were hurt. Her legs were fractured. They both sat on the ground in pains and shock. Passersby were trying to lift them to quickly get them to the hospital. I got my luggage and left the scene of the accident unhurt.

I pondered over what happened and was really grateful to God as I got home safely to recount the story to my family. It was Passover for me. It could have been my leg fractured had I argued with the girl over where I should have sat. I didn't claim my rights to where to sit. I chose to be foolish and God spared my life. I considered her a ransom for me.

I was sorry for the driver. I am not sure whether I remembered to give him his fare.

It dawned on me that I had narrowly escaped an accident or even death. I couldn't but worship God with some Bible texts:

> *Our soul is escaped as a bird out of the snare of the fowlers: the snare is broken, and we are escaped. Our help is in the name of the LORD, who made heaven and earth. Surely God delivered me from the snare of the fowler.*
>
> *Psalm 91:3*

3

Juicy but Dangerous

I was transferred to an organization which was in another city and didn't really like to go. A window to change the posting was open to me which I was trying to explore. My boss appreciated my work and wanted to give me a letter requesting for me to be retained in his office which I consented to.

As soon as I left his office that day, I lost my peace and somehow knew God urgently wanted my attention. I went quickly into a rest room. "Holy Spirit…what is the matter?" I asked. He responded that I had missed His will by wanting to remain in that organization when my time was up there, and I was to report that same day to the new one. I thanked God with mixed feelings and proceeded on my new posting.

A meeting welcoming the personnel had been arranged and I was just in time for it. I didn't like the organization at all. It was far different from where I was coming from, smaller in every ramification and was probably going to be an office run by one man. As I settled down for the meeting, the Holy Spirit told me that the boss was going to ask a question and I was to be the first to answer. He didn't tell me the question. I didn't know much about the organization except bits and pieces that I had picked up from people. Their website didn't offer much either. I prayed for the Holy Spirit's assistance as the meeting commenced with the introduction of new staff.

Then the question came. "You must have heard about our organization, what can we do to improve and move it forward? My hand was up before I could think; there was no other hand up. I found myself saying "image laundering". My new boss was very happy and thanked me for the courage to say that.

After the meeting, I was summoned by the Boss who to my amazement, requested that I join his think tank team especially to strategize for an image laundering campaign for the office. I was happy and thanked God for great and promising things ahead.

I finished my documentation and was to move to a very big office whose occupant was retiring in a couple of days. I was to take over his schedule which was what we called a *juicy* schedule. It was a powerful schedule that many envied. The man pleaded with me for a couple of days to conclude his handover note. That was very fine by me so I went to my direct boss and sought for permission to travel for two weeks to relocate my belongings.

I was gone for two weeks during which I received a phone call that the man I was to take over from had retired and submitted his hand over note to another colleague who had lobbied for the juicy position. I was upset at this development.

My husband was curious about the phone call and I narrated what transpired to him. To my surprise he said 'that wasn't your schedule otherwise nobody would have taken it and God may have better plans for you. On the other hand, the person had made a big mistake if it was actually your position he took'. That was quite philosophical. He advised that I settle the matter with God in prayer.

I had no proper office by the time I resumed work and had to settle for what I considered a store. I was not happy at all but I kept my cool. When I eventually met the colleague, Mr. Neb that lobbied for my office, I greeted him warmly as if nothing had happened.

Few weeks later, the organization was restructured, Neb's office was scrapped and his schedule was merged with mine. It was his turn to be distraught. His huge office became moribund when he was not reassigned a schedule for a couple of years. He had no work while I was overwhelmed with work. At my back, he grumbled and complained to all that cared to listen about management's favoritism for me. When he had no more ears to listen to his tales of woe, he became antagonistic. I however did not give him an opportunity to exchange words with me which was what he desperately wanted.

Neb, out of frustration lobbied to get a posting from our organization which turned out to be the beginning of his night mare. He bade all of us farewell and left. Unfortunately for him after several months, he was told that his new posting which was wrongly done had been reversed.

Our man was now hanging between two work places; the one that had released him and the other that rejected him. For months, he was stranded after which he decided to return to our office. Luckily for him, he had not submitted his office key and we were yet to do a send forth event for him.

It took him a lot of plea and time before he could be reabsorbed to our office where he had become a laughingstock.

In the meantime I was in charge of projects, travels and tours. Staff would come to lobby to be included in our projects. I became like a Joseph who was a clearing house for those who wanted to buy food in Egypt because God through Pharaoh had uplifted him in the land. I was also like Mordecai in the Bible who the king elevated and made to ride his horse majestically through the town while his enemy held the reins of the horse. Bible says in the Psalms…you anoint my head with oil, in the presence of my enemies and my cup runs over.

A project came up and God spoke to me to include Neb on it which I gladly did. I didn't inform him yet when to my surprise he showed up in my cubicle office. That was probably his first time of entering my office. I'm sure he must have been embarrassed that my office was like his store.

He had a sorry tale to tell. He couldn't pay his kids' school fees; he had a terminal sickness that was gulping his salary. His vehicle had also almost packed up. He was stranded financially and needed immediate bail out. I felt pity for him. I remembered how true my husband's admonition was to hand him over to God. I wanted to tell him to his face that he indeed made a mistake taking my job but I felt God had humbled him enough. It was his turn to be surprised when I told him he should consider his request done as I had put him on a project that would guarantee some allowances for him.

I became his friend as he gladly received instructions and assignments from me.

The big bang came when one day the Lord told me that they were going to give me a very delicate job going to a war zone which I was not to refuse. He also told me that Neb would be given the job but he would reject it. I was not to persuade him to take it up. I was quiet as we had a departmental meeting on the new task. He wasn't at the meeting. When my name came up to take up the task there was a general consensus that I was too overwhelmed with work to take up that assignment, also it was a man's task which should be given to Neb who never had a schedule. I didn't say a word at that meeting. Neb came after we had dispersed. Just as the Lord told me, he threw tantrums when he heard that they had given him a task at long last......a dangerous task for that matter. He abused whoever he could and rejected the assignment.

When we got to the management meeting, the overall boss who didn't know what had transpired at the departmental level suddenly announced the commencement of the assignment and had appointed me as task team leader. The departmental boss wanted to raise an objection to say how busy I was and that Neb should be directed to take it up. His voice was muffled by the Deputy boss who said that they had observed that my assignments so far had all been successful and he had come to a conclusion that my success factor could only have been God. The big boss ended the meeting by requesting me to get a brief on the task and to commence immediately.

The task became the juiciest of my assignments...... very dangerous, life threatening but rewarding. Neb was right. My small bosses were right that it was a man's job but God was with me.

The first task was a mission to rebels' camp. They had just surrendered and we were to profile them. We entered a war chopper in readiness for any attack but we landed safely in the midst of thousands of rebels. I was assigned the females and it was a terrible experience as I profiled even the girl rebels. Some of them were pregnant or had become mothers in their teenage. They were as wild as a bull and had no remorse that they were rebels. It wasn't an easy task as it was getting dark and we had to tactically retreat from there to a safer location.

After one of our visits, I had left in a chopper to another destination where we could do some paper work. A young soldier, who was a member of another team made room for me to go on the chopper as the first batch. We landed safely in readiness for work. I barely was at my desk when they radioed us that the chopper had crashed…and the other team members had died. I still recall the soldier's face as he stepped down for me to enter. I asked after him and they said 'nobody survived'. I remember clearly that we didn't get up from our seats but continued with our work; there was no minute silence and nobody mentioned it again as if we all agreed not to.

On another visit, we had entered a small fighter plane to a rebel zone. The plane landed in a small deserted airstrip from where we took a chopper to our destination. We were in the middle of nowhere and could not possibly sleep there but had to return to base before night fall. As we approached our small plane, I knew something was wrong but couldn't place a handle on it. The pilot greeted us but requested to use the gents somewhere, surprisingly the most senior man on the team also requested for a visit to the gents. I knew something was wrong so I signaled to my team member to follow them discretely.

My team member hurriedly returned to tell me that he heard them discussing that the plane was in a bad state and that it was high risk for him to fly it; but that the team lead was resolved that we had to take off in it.

The duo returned and pretended as if all was well. It was like a suicide mission. My team member was already sweating as we reluctantly entered the aircraft. I told him that the option we had was to pray. I said my prayers throughout the entire journey which was more than an hour. Others didn't know what was happening…they were talking, sleeping or requesting for some drinks or food. We were seven in number.

I will spare you the details but it could only have been God that spared our life. When we eventually landed, the team leader was too much in a state of shock that he just kept walking in some direction without saying a word to anyone. Nobody went after him. We went quietly in different directions wondering whether we were really alive or in a trance.

What kept me going was that God asked me to handle the task way before my boss did. I was sure that God's plans for me were not wicked. I recalled the Bible scripture:

> *"If you'll hold on to me for dear life," says GOD,*
> *"I'll get you out of any trouble. I'll give you the*
> *best of care if you'll only get to know and trust me.*
> *Call me and I'll answer, be at your side in bad times;*
> *I'll rescue you, and then throw you a party.*
> *Psalm 91:15 MSG*

I also recalled the saying of a man of God that "God is not committed to what He has not commanded'.

4

The Lucky Number

We were to accompany our CEO to a dinner that an Ambassador had invited us to. We had all looked forward to it and it turned out to be a very good outing. As we sat at his table, he informed us that as their custom, they would welcome guests with a game to know who was the luckiest among the twelve of us. Our hosts brought two small baskets with identical content. Numbers were written on some papers and rolled into a ball from which we were to pick a number. After we took numbers from the first basket, our chief host was given the second basket from which he was to pick the lucky number.

As soon as I opened my wrapped paper, I discovered that I took the Number three. I suddenly tuned to God's frequency and reminded him that I was His child and that three stands for Trinity hence it should be the lucky number. I told God that a gift may not be attached to the game but making me win would just be an indication of His love, support and presence with me. It was a speedy prayer before the Ambassador announced the number he had picked. It was Number Three.

I lost decorum as I jumped and shouted for joy. My boss was embarrassed at the way I shouted and behaved. He gave me a look that meant *can you get your art together, please?* I quickly repackaged myself to fit into his protocol.

Why was I glad? I wanted to dance as David in the Bible danced. It was a sign to me that God still answered prayers and that the omnipotent God was interested in the affairs of man. It was my communication to God in recognition of His faithfulness and love. I understood that God was interested in the details of our life; that some of His children at that dinner didn't bother to ask Him for favor but left the matter to chance; that we often believe that God should handle bigger things while we deal with smaller issues; and that we give up too soon with the attitude of whatever would be would be. I didn't take that event for granted nor explained it away as sheer coincidence.

In the Bible, Peter and his co-fishermen were all in the boat at night when Jesus walked on water to meet them. It was only Peter that dared to ask a question. "Lord, if it is you bid me come" and the Lord said 'come'. Peter actually arose and walked on top of water with his eyes fixed on Jesus. However, a boisterous storm arose which made him to shift his gaze from Jesus and he began to sink. In desperation, he cried out to Jesus for help and was rescued. I observed that he did not cry out to his fellow fishermen to rescue him but to Jesus who bade him come.

We often rely on friends, family, colleagues and government to bail us out when in trouble, only to be disappointed and embarrassed at the let down from them. There is no safety net anywhere except in Christ Jesus. All other ground is sinking sand.

God is not a gambler; He packages blessings for His children; and those that are willing to ask Him will get from Him.

5

Corpses and Graves

Only God can tell how many thousands of people showed up for a job interview that I was invited to. When it was almost midnight, I decided to forfeit the exercise and go home to my family because it was not yet my turn and it would be too late to get home. My house was an hour away by car and I didn't have a vehicle.

Just before I left, I pleaded with some of the officials that as a nursing mother I should be allowed to take the exam with the next batch of candidates. They obliged me. Afterwards, I rushed to pick my belongings and darted towards the staircase as the elevator had been shut down for the day.

A policeman suddenly stopped me as I got to the staircase, to make room for the CEO of the organization who was just leaving the office. I had seen the CEO on the television and pages of the newspaper but that was my first time of seeing him face to face. However, he waved at me to move on and I thanked him as I dashed down the staircase. That was my first encounter with the CEO. God bless my aunt who had arranged a vehicle to take me home in that dead of the night.

Thanks to God that I got the job.

A couple of years later, they initiated a program in the organization to give awards to hardworking officers, and I earned one of the awards. I met the CEO again for the second time as he shook hand with me and congratulated me on the award.

I worked in that office for many more years; the CEO's tenure expired and he left. Others came and left after him; and I became the head of the regional office. One day I got a call from headquarters that CEO had died abroad. His corpse would be flown home and I was to receive and keep it in custody until I was directed to release it to his family.

I went to the Arrival section of the airport in the company of my staff and waited earnestly for the corpse until I was informed to go to the cargo section. It was then it dawned on me that CEO had become a corpse cargo which could no longer come through the arrival hall. I ran to the cargo section and was stupefied as I watched it being lowered by a forklift. It was finally handed over to me in the presence of some of his relations and former colleagues. The corpse was deposited in a morgue. CEO was dressed in attire he would never have worn in his lifetime. He was lying there helpless as they carried out activities to preserve him. It was over.

I had a flash back to the day I first saw him when I had a peep at his face as he waved at me to take the staircase. The second time was seconds of opportunity to shake his hand and smile at the cameraman so I didn't get a good look at his face. This time around the situation was different. I had a long look at his face that had changed. I was in that pre morgue room with him for about thirty minutes. I watched as they dressed him up in new clothes that his family had brought for him. The morgue was heavily guarded as though the corpse would be stolen. I was very glad when the directives came that his family had fixed the date for his burial and I was to release his corpse to them.

I considered the role I played in receiving his corpse a dramatic irony. He never could have fathomed it that the same young girl whom he saw briefly on that interview night would be pertinent to his funeral. His tenure in life had ended. His life had expired.

Another bizarre event I experienced had to do with a widow I knew. Her husband had just died and I had the privilege of talking to her. She was distant and unreached as I spoke to her. She had entered a cocoon of grief and gloom that nobody could penetrate. She was in that state for more than a year before she started falling apart in sickness. At first she didn't care, she wanted to die. We cajoled her to be concerned about her children and to fight for her life but she was unperturbed. She was indeed torn between dying and living. It was when death stared her in the face and her pains became unbearable that she started seeking help. By then she was a shadow of herself – more like a ghost and it was too late to save her life. When she died, we tried to reach her in-laws but they were uncooperative neither did her own family show up.

Eventually a group of friends gathered some money together and organized a service of songs as part of the funeral rites. The next day, some of the friends and her children took her corpse to her village for burial. The roads were bad and they arrived at the village late in the night but before they could enter the village, some vehicles with hoodlums overtook the ambulance that was carrying the corpse, caused some chaos and kidnapped the corpse.

Our friends who went for the proposed burial were shocked and didn't know what to do. They put a call through and we advised them to report the matter to the police as well as her family. There was pandemonium in the village. Our delegates could not understand the dialect that was spoken and the children had gone their different ways. They eventually found a place to sleep and left the village first thing the next morning.

What became of the corpse?

We learnt that the relatives of the woman abducted the corpse as protest against their in-laws; and demanded for some levy before the corpse was finally released to be laid to rest. There wasn't any further explanation. It was over. She had returned to her maker.

Shortly before I left that job, I also received the corpse of a woman who was battered by bullets from armed robbers. She embarked on a night journey of about twelve hours when the bus she was travelling in was attacked. The bullet penetrated her face and came out from the back of her head. She was hit before the driver could raise an alarm.

Her wealthy husband was distraught at the sight of the corpse but was screaming at the kind of cheap casket that was almost falling apart in which the corpse was handed over to him. I didn't know what to say to him…. He was obviously confused and frustrated as he told me all the plans he had for his wife, his wealth and why on earth his wife took a night bus when she could afford to chatter an aircraft. I had no response for him. It was over.

On another occasion, I watched a woman as she received the corpse of her husband. The man had just submitted his retirement letter and was given a last assignment to lead a delegation to some regions of the country. This gesture afforded him an opportunity to make some money to support him before his pension sailed through. The assignment turned out to be his last assignment indeed. His colleagues found his corpse in his hotel room.

I watched as his wife spoke to the corpse as if he could hear her. She narrated how she had endured his being away working in a different city far away from home; and how she waited patiently for his retirement from office and looked forward to his return home to his family. One thing I remembered she told him was that death was not on the agenda they ever discussed while they planned for his retirement. It was over sooner than she expected.

Another strange event I recall was that of an elderly friend of mine who invited us to officiate at her mother's funeral. Everything went well until we got to the burial site. She had given money to some relatives to help secure a burial space for her mother. Unfortunately the grave given was like a dumpsite for corpses. We were walking on skeletons and bones to get to the site. Some people must have turned back but as ministers we had a duty to perform.

It was a shallow grave where an attendant was evacuating a corpse that was buried in it earlier. It was probably just a ceremonial grave. I watched as the attendant used some grave clothes to evacuate bones out of the grave. It was a gory sight but I had to support my friend whose mother we were there to bury. She solicited advice if she could postpone the burial while she sourced for another burial site but nobody supported her.

Almost a third of the casket was above ground level by the time we finished the interment. I consoled her that she had taken care of her mother very well while she was alive which was what mattered.

My friend was very embarrassed that day. She explained that her relatives whom she trusted to handle the interment had let her down and probably duped her. We eventually left the burial site with different imaginations of what would happen to that corpse within an hour of our departure. We learnt that there were different nocturnal commercial activities that normally happen at the burial ground. Life was over and a funeral had taken place.

6

The Hospital Saga

I was at the female surgical ward of a hospital to talk about Jesus Christ to the patients. There was a young girl in her early twenties who had just undergone a surgery. I learnt she just lost her baby from a caesarean operation. Her fiancé who cuddled her was really distraught but tried to act like a man.

Some young doctors who came to her bedside to review her case encouraged her that she would soon be discharged from the hospital. Few minutes later, I heard the same doctors instructing the nurses on duty to hand her over to counselors who would break the news of her AIDS status to her and her fiancé. The girl didn't know she had AIDS. AIDS was like a death sentence at that time. Both of them were still in grief about the loss of their baby and were oblivious of the more sad news that awaited them.

I watched as her fiancé helped to sit her up and encouraged her to take a cup of tea. She was drinking the tea when she suddenly screamed. The suture on her stomach had ruptured. Her intestines were out visibly and water started pouring out of her stomach. I saw it clearly. It was like gutter waters...black and smelly.

People ran out of the ward while those who couldn't run covered their noses. I watched as the girl used one hand to scoop her intestines and the other to cover her own nose. I cannot recollect what the boy did. The nurses quickly wore their gloves and headed for her bed which they quickly condoned while the attendants cleaned up and disinfected the place. I went out for fresh breath as I heard people gather to discuss the matter. I really felt sorry for the boy. It was too much for him. We watched as she was quickly wheeled back to the theatre for a re-suturing.

I was there when they wheeled her back. She was alive. She had overcome that crisis...still she didn't know that the worse news was yet to come. I left without having an opportunity to tell them about the capabilities of Jesus and wondered what became of them.

In the same ward, I met a teenager that was just being discharged from the hospital. She was young, beautiful but lousy. She also was an AIDS patient. She was a regular patient in that ward and almost everyone knew her. She boasted about the many guys she had slept with and many more she would have sex with. She was scruffy, shameless and untroubled. Her mother and aunt who were with her were distressed as they helped her to put her belongings in a bag. I really felt pity for the mother who obviously had raised a wild rose as a child.

There was another case of a woman in her early forties in the ward. She was in high spirit as she came into the ward and took her bed. I watched as she arranged her stuff in her bedside cupboard. She was an extrovert and we soon got talking. I spent a long time trying to tell her about Jesus and the benefits of serving God. I learnt she was separated from her husband and had painstakingly brought up her son who was a teenager.

She was in high spirit on the day of her surgery but I noticed that there were no relatives or friends with her. She was all alone. The surgery took longer than usual and I was already wondering what was happening. Patients were usually quiet after surgery but I heard her voice from a distance as they wheeled her back to the ward. The surgery on her didn't go well.

She came back with tubes all over her....blood and water. She was writhing in pains. I felt very sorry for her. I learnt from the nurses that her intestines and some internal things were ruptured mistakenly.

There was still no relative or friend with her. She was lamenting and kept asking a rhetoric question...*who would take care of her son*? She knew she wasn't going to make it. She repeated that question uncountable times before she became quiet. I stayed with her pleading with her to give her life to Christ if she believed she would not make it....but each time, she asked me who would take care of her son. She was too concerned about her son to grab the opportunity to give her life to Christ.

I wondered why they didn't correct the mistake in the theatre but learnt later that they had sent for a specialist who was to come the next day. Unfortunately, the woman didn't make it till the next day. We just saw that she was covered up and wheeled out. The boy's name was in her mouth till she passed on. It was over. There was still no friend or relative.

I can tell people about the capability of Jesus to save, heal and deliver from oppression. I was prone to Malaria but I had a covenant with God not to have it and I never did for more than ten years. Also, my sight was bad and had three specs. My child challenged me one day to pray to God concerning it. The God who prevented me from having Malaria fever can heal my bad sight, he said. The God of the Mountain is also the God of the valley. The God who can prevent can also cure. By the time we finished the conversation, my faith rose up and I prayed again desperately to God to heal me. I was healed instantly. This has been more than fifteen years. I have also experienced more financial blessings, fruitful opportunities and promotions that could only have been by God. I can boldly thank God and say that I didn't earn them....they just fell on my laps.

7

The Strange Giant

I was in a prayer camp on a retreat. It was dead in the night when suddenly I opened my eyes and saw a strange giant creature by my bedside. He was furious, daring and intimidating. It was apparent he wanted to attack me but could not. He was angry and wanted to move just a little bit further but could not. Some higher power must have restrained him from carrying out his wickedness. He growled like an animal while I helplessly watched the scene. I could not even shout the name of Jesus. I was just mute.

I watched as he later turned his back on me and started moving towards the window of the room. He didn't turn his back like a human being would do. His back was just turned in a second. He went away still vibrating and flexing muscles as a demonstration of displeasure at not fulfilling his assignment. He disappeared as soon as it got to the window.

I slowly got up from the bed to put on the light while whispering the name of Jesus. I stayed the rest of the night praying.

Most people that died in their sleep were said to have died of cardiac arrest. I realized from that experience that they could have died from unpleasant encounters with forces of darkness. They just didn't survive the experience to tell their story.

I had just finished a session of prayer before sleeping when that demonic entity showed up. I pondered what could have happened had I not prayed at all. I mused over all these possibilities and came to conclusion that it was not by power or might that I survived it but the mercies of God that rescued me.

The Bible text that 'except the Lord watches over a city the watchmen watch in vain' is right. Very appropriate is another Bible text that 'our weapons of warfare are not carnal but mighty through God to the pulling down of strongholds...for we wrestle not against flesh and blood but against principalities and powers and spiritual wickedness in high places....for the devil comes but to steal, kill and destroy'. From these Bible texts, I understood better that nobody can really secure his life except God grants the grace.

8

Divine Rescue

We gave one of our vehicles to someone to use for a while till he repaired his own but it was taking too long for him to return the car. One day, I needed to use the car for school run and we had to call him to return the car. I wasn't at home when he returned it hence he left the keys with someone.

I somehow suspected foul play and had a restraint from entering the vehicle or even touching its keys. I called one of our old pastors to express my fears. He also could discern that something was wrong. He told me not to enter the vehicle because it had been jinxed. I found that hard to believe. We had a session of prayer on phone and I was directed to 'watch and pray' for a couple of days.

I took a cab instead of using the vehicle that day. After I left, I received news that our driver came to take the vehicle for school run and had an accident....it was a miracle that nobody died. I called my pastor and told him what happened and was shocked when he said that the jinx was still on the vehicle. The vehicle was badly damaged and had to be towed to a mechanic garage. I thought the vehicle would become a scrap but somehow the mechanics were able to put it back to shape after several months. When it was ready, the driver picked it up from the garage and did school run with it the same day.

Few hours later I received a phone call from him that he was involved in another accident....a bullion van had run them over and sped off. Once again all the children came out unhurt but the vehicle was badly damaged...and towed back to the mechanic's garage the same day.

I learnt that the jinx on the vehicle was labeled and targeted like a guided missile. I would have died instantly if I had been in the vehicle.

I thanked God for giving us men of God as gifts, and the hunch of the Holy Spirit to expose the plans of the enemy as well as keep us from danger. Indeed if it had not been the Lord on my side, I would have been a minced meat for the enemy.

Another incident I need to thank God for: I drove a vehicle to a town not too far away for an event that lasted three days. I drove back home with about eight people in the car. I was just overtaking a trailer on a hilly portion of the road when suddenly the engine of my vehicle went off. I lost control of the vehicle and didn't know what to do. All I remembered was that people were screaming the name of Jesus in the vehicle.

In the midst of that confusion, an invincible hand took over the steering and drove it up the hill for about five minutes. It was like drama to me as the vehicle was driven off the road and parked by the fence of a church. I didn't see the hand but my hand was barely on the steering and the engine of the car was off. We all came out thanking God and took another vehicle home.

The mechanic that later went to check it came back with a scary tale - the engine of the vehicle had broken to pieces as if it was hit by a high impact truck. It was towed to the mechanics.

My conclusion was that a life without Christ was highly susceptible to sudden death and evil.

I will share another divine escapade I had. I just finished a prayer vigil in my home and quickly prepared to go to work in the early hours of the morning. I had an official driver which made it convenient for me to usually sleep after such vigils in the vehicle. I could sleep off as I entered the vehicle till I got to the office which was about an hour.

On this occasion, as I was about entering the vehicle, the Lord told me to place my right hand on my seat before sitting on it. I didn't think twice or asked for reasons. I just obeyed.

However, when I got to my office, God told me that the driver had been stalking me spiritually and wanted to put a jinx on me severally but didn't succeed. I didn't believe that because he was a very good driver...courteous, seemingly godly, well - dressed and mannered. I politely told God that I found it hard to believe and apologized for my unbelief.

God was patient with me as He gave me privileged information about the driver.

The driver was not the religious person he claimed to be but a member of a strong cult in his hometown. As the boss, he assumed I was very rich and had a huge account at work; and wanted to put me under his spell to take the money at will. I could also become his sexual partner anytime he willed.

He was worried that his jinx attempts on me had failed repeatedly and had given a situation report at his coven where he sourced for alternatives. He was therefore summoned to come physically to a night meeting for a higher ritual.

He would seek my approval for a week casual leave to attend to some urgent matters in his hometown. I was to grant him his request.

I was shocked to hear all this and still expressed my doubts. God had more to say. At his cult meeting, they planned to summon my spirit to the meeting and give it instructions that couldn't be disobeyed. I became afraid. I had never heard such a thing in my life. God told me not to fear. If they dared invoke my spirit another person would answer and die.

I didn't believe God. I thought I was hallucinating until few minutes later I heard a knock on my door. It was the same driver that came in to seek approval to travel to his town.

The coincidence was too much. I immediately gave him the approval he wanted but probed into what he was going home to do. He lied that he was the head of his clan and was invited to settle some tribal squabbles before it degenerated. I asked who was going to relieve him and he mentioned a driver nicknamed *soap grinder*.

After two weeks, my driver returned with grey hair and unkempt beard. He apologized for not returning to work in few days like he promised…reason being that he lost his daughter.

What happened? I asked.

He narrated in a sober mood that he was in the middle of a town meeting somewhere when he received an urgent call that his daughter had slumped and died instantly. I asked how old the daughter was and he said that she was already married. She slumped at her husband's feet. I asked if she had been sick and he said no. He had seen her before going for his meeting.

As soon as he left my office I went on my knees to thank God and rolled on the floor in appreciation for rescuing me from bondage and destruction. If his spell had succeeded, he would have ruined my life, home marriage, work, ministry and everything.

I thanked God for not allowing diabolic men to gain advantage over me.

God spoke loud and clear again to me that the battle was yet to be over. He told me that the driver now believed that I was a strong witch that killed his daughter. He was ready to revenge that same day. His plan was to drive me into the sea in a planned accident while he would use a popular African charm that would transport him safely from the accident scene to his room or some specified place.

I asked God what to do.

He informed me that the driver had already jinxed the vehicle but I was to enter it after close of work and play along. I became scared but God assured me that He just wanted the driver to believe he was winning before He judged him.

However, I was to ensure he didn't drive the vehicle and I was to keep praying in the vehicle.

At the close of work, I strategically collected the car keys from him and told him to take some time off after his bereavement. He was disappointed and soberly went to his seat as he couldn't argue with me. I asked *soap grinder* to drive me instead. I combined both faith and fear as *soap grinder* sped off.

God had told me that the battle location was on a popular bridge. As soon as we got there, an invincible power picked up the vehicle as if it was a match box and moved it thrice towards the railings of the bridge to drop it in the sea.

The vehicle did not somersault yet we were at the railing of the bridge. I was too overwhelmed to talk.

Soap grinder took a long look at me and to my surprise said, 'if your driver wants to kill you, must he kill me his colleague as well? I will deal with him and prove to him that they don't call me *soap grinder* for nothing'

I was now dumbfounded. I couldn't belief it that he knew what was happening.

Something was wrong with the vehicle that it could not start. *Soap grinder* opened the bonnet and started speaking some gibberish incantation to it. After a while the engine picked and I heard him say to himself that it was important for him to drive the vehicle to our destination but that it would be suicidal for any vehicle to hit ours. I didn't understand that but didn't ask questions since he was soliloquizing and communicating with his demons. I was thanking my God who is the head of all principalities and powers. He concentrated on his driving and never said a word till I got home.

Both drivers had different powers and spirits they conjured and believed in and they understood themselves. Once again the Lord rescued me…from ignorance, vulnerability and death.

The following week my driver lost another child. It was his grown up son that had a good job somewhere.

Thanks to God who reveals secrets to his children like He did to Daniel, Joseph, Elisha, amongst others in the Bible. I appreciated the day I handed over the steering wheel of my life to Jesus otherwise I would have been a cheap prey to my employees and their demons.

9

Helper at Hand

Several years ago in Lagos Nigeria, I was struggling to enter a *kabukabu (cab)* with some other people because it had just a space for only one person left popularly referred to as *one chance* and I counted myself lucky to have entered the vehicle.

But no sooner was I thanking God for the vehicle than I realised that I was the only female in the vehicle while the others were not looking particularly friendly.

I refused to give in to fear as I recalled stories about the notorious *one chance* vehicles usually linked to kidnapping, robbery and rituals.

Suddenly, the man that was sitting next to me spoke aggressively to me to wind down the window glass. Then I realised that the window pane was up and that the winder had been removed. I immediately sensed trouble and danger.

Like a lamb, I replied the man that the winder was not there but to my suprise, the driver bellowed a command 'take it from her!

I had only a small purse which was on my laps and there was not much money in it. I expected them to snatch the purse but the man that sat beside me suddenly put his hand round my neck to strangulate me.

The car sped off my course into some deserted area. I was stuggling to breath or to remove my head from the man's grip when suddenly God spoke to me.

He said 'start speaking in tongues aloud' with emphasis on the word *aloud.*

I was choking but managed to begin to speak out in tongues.

The driver repeated his command to his colleague to take *it* from me and I realized that they were not after the purse which was still on my laps.

I was about to panic when the man oppressing me replied the driver.

He said, 'I can't touch her'.

I was confused because his hand was on my neck but his confession of failure was an encouragement to me that God was with me.

Then God spoke again to me.

'Tell them to drop you in Jesus name' - the emphasis this time was on *Jesus name.*

I managed to say out 'drop me in Jesus name.'

The driver slammed his foot on the breaks and the car was forced to a halt. I was quickly shoved out of the vehicle and the car sped off.

Things happened so fast that I could not take note of the make or colour of the vehicle. In fact, I thought I was having a bad dream.

I observed that I was in an area that I had never been before and the only person I saw was an elderly man who directed me on how to get out of the area. I followed his directions and suddenly burst out at one of the usual hustle and bustle streets of Lagos.

I have recounted this story to several people but never had the courage to say that I was strangely transported to that hustle and bustle street of Lagos. I didn't walk to that street; I just found myself on it. One minute I was with the elderly man that gave me directions and the next minute I was on that busy street. I stongly believe that the elderly man I saw was an angel of the Lord. I found a semblance in the Bible where Philip was divinely transported from Gaza to Azotus.

> *And when they were come up out of the water,*
> *the Spirit of the Lord caught away Philip, that*
> *the eunuch saw him no more: and he went on*
> *his way rejoicing. But Philip was found at Azotus*
> Act 8:39-40

My heart was racing as I played back the event in my mind. What was the man commanded to take from me? But my purse was on my laps which they did not even touch; they must have wanted something precious to me that I didnt know about; but it seemed the man was trying to snuff out my life; what exactly was their mission?

Thank God I didn't witness their mission. But I now know it could not have been less than to steal, kill and destroy.

You may say that I was lucky. Some others might not have been that lucky. But I really appreciate God for intercepting their evil plan and that I could hear His voice on that day.

I thought about it. What an irony that often times we argue with God, ignore His instructions, neglect and defy Him and seem to get away with it repeatedly but hardly can you find anyone who will argue with armed robbers, ritualists and death.

10

Poisoned

I used to go to a restaurant early in the morning to eat before getting to work. The meals there were so sumptuous that rich people parked their state of the art vehicles by the road to hustle for a seat in the restaurant; some even had to stand with food in their hands waiting for a vacant seat. I enjoyed the meals and almost became addicted to it.

One day the Lord spoke to me never to eat at that restaurant again. I didn't ask why but I reluctantly obeyed. I pity those who still eat there.

I discovered another *joint* (smaller restaurant) closer to my office and started ordering food from there. One day as I settled to eat, a friend came in and found the food enticing.

He said that he wasn't interested in the meal which was rice and asked if he could just take a piece of meat. I quickly obliged. He used my spoon to pick the meat which he put in his mouth and then dropped the empty spoon in my food. I didn't see anything wrong in that since he was a friend.

However after he left, I took the spoon to continue eating my food. I scooped some rice from the dish and ate it. To my surprise when I swallowed it, it was as if I swallowed a big meat and not rice. I knew immediately that I was in trouble and that my friend had contaminated the meal spiritually. He had converted my rice to something evil. I quickly poured the food away but the deed was already done. I couldn't vomit whatever it was.

I became very restless and almost died that day as energy was fast depleting from me. Suddenly my pastor brother called from a long distance and wanted to know if I was alright. From his house he sensed that I was in some trouble and was praying. He told me to quickly leave the place and start heading home while he would be in prayers till I got home. By the time I got home, he was already in my house interceding for me. It was only by the mercies of God that I escaped that attack. It was not a condition that could be diagnosed physically otherwise I would have headed for the hospital.

Few days later, I learnt that my friend was a member of a dangerous cult but God was steps ahead of him. From that day I began to decree the blood of Jesus over any food I'm served.

I had another restaurant encounter. It was close to my house and the owner was a widow who had gone through several ordeals after her husband's demise. She was respectful and hardworking. Her restaurant was always packed full with people who loved the local food she cooked.

One day she saw my niece on the streets and asked after me. It had been a while she had seen me she said. When the girl told her I was home, she volunteered to give me the food I liked free of charge. I quickly sent a big dish to her for the food but was very disappointed when the girl brought back just a small portion of food which was barely enough to eat. I quickly sat down to eat the food after praying on it.

Few weeks later I heard from a reliable source that she was directed by some diviners to give me food that was charmed so that she could achieve pregnancy for one of her daughters. Unfortunately it didn't work. Hence she tried to send someone close to me to inquire whether I ate the food or not. Eventually the cat was let out of the bag. The next time the woman saw me she took to her heels.

I was thankful to God who just gave me free food to eat because it is written in the Bible that when you are in Christ, deadly things and poison would not hurt you. It is also in the Bible that many are the afflictions of the righteous but the Lord delivers him from them all.

Another saga was during a New Year festive period. I had travelled and left some of my wards at home. Someone they knew brought food for me and were happy to eat it since I wasn't around. They however left some portion for the *Buzu mai'guard* …security man at the gate. After they had finished their meal the *Buzu* who was always happy to be fed by us came running and shouting to them not to eat the food. He had thrown both food and plate away; it was charmed food which must not be eaten.

The Buzus are non Nigerians used as cheap security men who are well known for their fetish lifestyle. It was believed that they could turn to animals to fight their opponents. They are very efficient that armed robbers and thieves always evade the houses where they watch.

My wards called me to report that they had eaten poison and were apprehensive that they might not live to see the next day. I first of all rebuked them for lack of sensitivity... why should it be a *Buzu* to tell them that a food was poisoned...and not the other way round. However I assured them that they would not die because there is provision for such mistakes in the Bible....*if you take any poison, it shall by no means hurt you.* I told them that scripture would work for them if they had faith. They survived by the Word of God.

11

Price for Two-Timing

I had a colleague who was very quiet and modest. She was young, beautiful and could be referred to as a good Christian --she was always attending church fellowships. One day, she announced to us that she would soon be getting married and we were all quite happy for her in the office because her colleagues in her age range were married.

The wedding day approached and she took her leave from work to enable her plan for the celebration. A day or two before her leave commenced, she asked me jokingly what gift I would give to her and I also replied jokingly that she deserved a freezer. That same day we spoke, she took a commercial vehicle to her place and disembarked at her bus stop and was about to cross the freeway when suddenly she was dead. She was run over by a bullion van and dragged a distance because the vehicle was at top speed. The police came and deposited her mangled body in the morgue. Few days later we were informed of her demise and it was sorrow at work. When we asked where they put her, the response was 'freezer'. I became afraid of God.

The groom to be was grief stricken. He was the pastor of her church and the whole congregation was already preparing for the wedding ceremony. He came to the office to see some of us and blubbered like a child. He was a very tall and handsome man and some of us were seeing him for the first time. He came to tell us the arrangements for the funeral and that his church would take absolute responsibility. We consoled him and prayed for God's comfort while we wondered how he would pick up the pieces of life he thought he had figured out. We almost took offence at God for allowing such evil to happen to a pastor.

Two days later and to our utmost surprise, a man and a girl showed up in our office. We thought we saw a ghost because the girl was a carbon copy of our friend that died; she was wearing one of her clothes and was about the same height with the deceased. At closer look, we saw that she was a younger version of our colleague, probably her younger sister.

I started hearing whispers. What s going on? The man introduced himself to us as the husband of the deceased and the girl was their daughter. We were confused. When we put the bits and pieces of information together, we realized that our colleague was married and had a child. Her family was in the village while she had come to the city to start a new life. She never mentioned it to any one of us nor the pastor-groom. We could have sworn that she was a virgin. We were too shocked to process the story. He was also a very tall and handsome man but a villager. She must have had a penchant for tall and handsome men. He also came to tell us about the funeral arrangements back home in the village and to solicit for assistance from the office. It was confusion as staff of our organization trooped out to see the daughter and husband.....in disbelief.

I learnt the Pastor later heard the truth. I'm sure he would have quickly wiped his tears and began to thank God for exposing the deceit and trap of an adulterous woman. It was still a shame though but I'm sure the church also celebrated the faithfulness of God to their Pastor and judgement on the impostor not minding what they had expended on the wedding preparation. She had guts to deceive a man of God. We wondered what would have happened if the Pastor discovered the truth a couple of days after their elaborate wedding ceremony. What a shame.

Integrity, honesty or truthfulness are part of the fruit of the Spirit which we should manifest as Christians. Old things should pass away and all things should become new. We are all work in progress in God's hands but we have a role to play too----to work out our salvation with fear and trembling---and not to be pointed out as bad eggs of the family of God.

12

The Spider's Web

A boy happily informed my friends and me that he had just got a job somewhere and was glad about it. He was happy that the job required not much stress. He would report at his boss's house who would give him some money to deposit in the bank. That was all his duty – to take money to the bank every day. He had no clue to the kind of job the man was doing because he rarely left the house but money was available every morning to be taken to the bank.

We sensed trouble and started asking him more questions about his boss. We knew the boy had entered a spider's web. We concluded that the boy was the victim and he didn't know it. We discerned that money was spiritually being siphoned from him each time he went to his house and he was actually depositing his virtues in the bank unknowingly. We asked if he wanted the truth. Of course he said yes and we told him the truth, counseled him to leave the job immediately and never return to the place, but he disputed it. He had searched for a job for years and this was a breakthrough for him. It would at least meet his immediate needs.

We sympathized with him and told him that our duty was to tell him the truth irrespective of what he thought. He did not believe us. He was pensive for a while and left.

He however discussed the issue with someone who told him not to discontinue the job. We told him that his celebrated breakthrough could become his breakdown and he should wait for God's time to give him a better job. He was not even earning a fantastic salary but stipends. He ignored our admonition and continued the job.

I ran into him almost a year later and was happy to see him looking good - he had gotten a regular job in a better place but to my surprise, he burst into tears pleading for help. He was very sick and dying inside. Something was obviously wrong with him. He could not label it but he felt that he was empty within - like an empty bottle. He had gone to hospitals but nothing was diagnosed. He tried to explain to people but nobody understood him. He was suffering in silence and alone. He needed deliverance from captivity of the devil.

His new job made him to be envied by his friends. Then the news came.....he was back on the streets jobless. He had been quietly relieved of his job because he was unwell and manifesting some strange behavior that was inimical to the image of the organization he worked for.

The Bible has it that there is a way that seems right to a man but it leads to death and hell. God promises to lead us in the way we are to go and guide us with his eyes.

I learnt that not all open doors are from God; it is only the blessing of God that lasts and gives peace and that God's time is always the best.

Furthermore in Acts of the Apostles (16:16), Paul had an encounter with a young girl who operated the spirit of divination. She had owners who were using her to make much money. The girl was possessed by an evil spirit that told people everything about them. I imagined that they took her to common places like markets where there were many so that she could tell them their past, present and future in return for money. Bible says that these men made much money by exploiting the girl's situation but when she saw Paul, she started following them for days declaring that they were servants of God.

Even though she was saying the truth about Paul and his colleagues, Paul knew it was the devil speaking and dealt with the foul spirit in the girl—and she was free. The owners were mad because their source of illegal income was over. The poor girl was taken advantage of rather than being helped.

I think we ought to learn a lesson from this incident especially nowadays that people flock around fake prophets, palm readers, horoscopes, herbalists and diviners who can tell them their future. I counsel you not to allow 'smart alecks' take advantage of you. The fact that someone says something true concerning you does not mean that person is of God. Stop running after voices that will lead you to destruction and hell. Give your life to Christ, study the scriptures and you will not be deceived by anybody.

I recalled my mother's song:

> *My father is the driver that is driving my vehicle*
> *He knows that I am in the vehicle*
> *He takes it easy as He drives me*
> *He will not let me enter a ditch (the ditch of life)*
> *My father is the one driving the vehicle of my life.*

13

The Occult Landlords

One of my friends graduated from college and decided to settle in Lagos. Her parents lived in the village but had a block of flats in Lagos which they leased to people. They reserved one of the flats for their use whenever they came to Lagos which was occasional. My friend knew where they kept the keys and she moved into the house.

She was not on good terms with her parents because she became born again. They were traditionalists and resented her faith. I am not sure if she got her parents' consent before she moved into the house. One day she invited her brethren in church to hold a vigil in the house. Her fiancé was also at the vigil. At the vigil, there was revelation that they were in a haunted house. The Holy Spirit revealed that a lot of things had been buried in the house and its compound with the purpose of siphoning the glory and blessings of the occupants in the compound. No wonder the tenants worked very hard but couldn't pay their meager rents. They were fruitless and unproductive. That was the case for all the tenants yet they didn't suspect foul play. Their landlord was the best thing that happened to them; he had listening ears to their tales of financial woe; his rents were the cheapest in the neighborhood and he didn't throw them out even when they could not pay the rents any longer.

Specific location that things were buried was revealed to the brethren who were audacious to prove the Word of God. They dug through the night and saw various strange things hidden in the walls and everywhere which they brought out and burnt. The brethren left the house in the early hours of the morning after the exercise.

To my friend's surprise, her father who rarely came to Lagos showed up just after the brethren left. He was furious that they had vandalized his house and screamed curses at his daughter as he threw her things out of his house. He was mad at his daughter for bringing brethren who could not mind their own business and who were audacious to tamper with what he had done. I am not sure if the tenants were privy to what happened.

My friend was homeless and didn't know what to do. She put a call through to her fiancé to give him an update but the brother did not pick her calls - it was very much unlike him.

Her fiancé narrated to the brethren how he was beaten up in his sleep by strange beings at night. He woke up with swollen eyes as well as badly bruised and battered body. He was also warned of his impending doom if he proceeded to marry the lady. He ran for his dear life.

We comforted her that her fiancé was not ordained to be her husband otherwise he would not have run. Some said that the fiancé was not living right with God and that was why he was the only victim of the backlash of what they did. People said different things to justify or condemn the boy's action. After few weeks, it became obvious to my friend that their relationship was over.

I wanted to attend her marriage a couple of years later but couldn't make it. She got married to a Pastor in her church. In spite of what the Pastor was told by several people, he was adamant that God told him to marry her. Together, they would put up a common front against forces of darkness and possibly rescue the souls of her parents from hell. Their mantra was that all things are possible with God.

I also remember a brother who was about getting married and needed to move from the slum he was living in. He was ashamed of that slum. The street gutters usually overflowed and found their way into his room. In his desperation, he got a better apartment which he quickly paid for and collected the keys. He was sure of a good relationship with his landlord.

The brother invited me to pray over the new house and I was excited to do so. We drove some distance to get to the house but no sooner had I come down from the vehicle than the Holy Spirit instructed me not to pray at all over the house.

The brother excitedly opened the doors while I tried to read God's mind. The instructions were clear not to attempt to say a word of prayer in the house. He took me through the apartment and I commented that it was beautiful. It was empty as he had not moved in yet.

He then brought out a bottle of anointing oil from his pocket since he observed that I didn't have mine. It was time to pray. I quickly changed the topic and asked if we could leave the house. It was a good house but God had rejected it without any explanation. I evaded his questions and he was stunned when I told him we should take our leave. When we got to the car, he asked again why I didn't pray and I responded that I didn't just feel like praying.

The next day, the landlord sent for him to return his keys and collect a refund.

"Why? What did I do wrong? Please tell me if you want a price increase", the brother pleaded with the landlord who insisted he didn't want his money or his presence in his house again. The brother concluded that the man was in the occult. He returned his keys and got his refund immediately.

The brother got married and took his bride to the slum where they lived come rain or shine; gutter waters or not. He had spent a lot on his wedding and had no money left. His young wife wasn't working. Things were rough but they endured it.

A couple of years later someone moved out of an apartment on his street and he quickly took it over with joy. This time there was no restraint about praying over the house. They lived happily and gave birth to their children in that house.

God is good and averts evil for us at different stages of the devil's plan. Being on God's side is a surety of His support when the devil comes knocking on our doors. The essence of coming to Christ and belonging to a Bible based church is to learn submission to God and how to resist the devil.

14

Appointment with Death

I was in a hospital to see a friend and had the privilege of entering the offices and consulting rooms. Just then a man was brought in bleeding and almost naked. I could hear his voice from far away. There were many people that came with him which was a problem for the nurses to handle. His case was really bad.

He was pleading with the doctors not to allow him to die. He obviously was a rich man from the remains of the clothes on him. I drew near to the family members to inquire what happened to him. The man had travelled to a town for an event which went on late into the night. He dismissed the driver and decided to drive back. He obviously slept off because the car somersaulted and went down a gorge in that late hour of the night. Unfortunately no vehicle was in sight hence the accident was unnoticed.

He was flung out of the vehicle into the deep and thick forest where he was throughout that night.

I wondered what went on his mind. Maybe he passed out and became conscious later. He was probably bitten by soldier ants and different kinds of insects. He could have heard different noises and movement of different animals typical of such a forest. There was no sign of the accident from the road. There were no mobile telephones then hence his family waited in vain for his arrival. They concluded that he must have slept in a hotel in the town he went.

When he didn't show up, the family became worried and got in touch with the organizers of the event who reliably told them when he left the party. Immediately his family most especially his wife panicked. They knew that he wasn't a *go-go* type and couldn't have been enjoying himself somewhere in the arms of ladies of easy virtue. They therefore began a search for him. They inquired at the police stations if there had been an accident; they assigned people to travel the same road whether they could locate probably the wreckage of his car. I don't know how many times they travelled that road in vain. It was night fall and they returned home without a clue to his whereabouts.

Meanwhile our man had become conscious but could not move his limbs. He was under his vehicle but could still breathe. He had been hopeful that help would come with daylight but night time was fast coming. I can imagine that he was disappointed, helpless and getting weaker. The family he much cherished and slaved for was not there to help him in his dare moments. He was left alone with his maker – God. He must have prayed earnestly to God perhaps in whispers to help him - at least for his corpse to be discovered and given a befitting burial. His only hope in that God forsaken thick forest was God.

God where are you? Please help me! Please send help to me!

God who is very kind- gave him many hours to live; he was watching and waiting. God says 'Cry unto me in the day of trouble and I will answer you'

The man must have recalled how rich he was; his several accounts probably in different currencies or the many loans he took. Is this how it would end? His children; his Will he had or not written; his wife – what would happen to her; his properties and business empire; his mother at home... how would she receive the news....she would be distraught; his siblings and dependants.

Is this really the end? God, please send help to me!

He could even have made series of vows unto God.... *if you help me God, I would go to church religiously with my wife and build a cathedral for you; I would do this and that.*

A dying man can be quite a desperate man.

Is my time up? Another harrowing night for me.....the noise of the creatures has started again.......oh.

It was morning again. It was a miracle that he survived another night. It was now the third day that he had been helpless in the forest without food and water, loosing blood and no help in sight.

Can God really hear, does he really answer prayers?

Suddenly he heard a noise from a far distance......and earnestly prayed to God this time for intervention. He couldn't even shout for help as he was trapped under his car. The noise grew louder and louder until they reached him.

A palm wine tapper had cited the vehicle in the forest from his vintage point on the palm tree. He quickly came down and walked some distance to alert policemen of his discovery. Help was already on his way while he was still in doubt about God. God sent a palm wine tapper to answer the prayer of a troubled man and his family. They had to cut through the forest to reach him. They secured more help to lift the vehicle off him. Some parts of his body were mangled but he could still narrate his tale of woe to the people. He forgot completely that he had money and precious documents in his briefcase but thanked God that he was brought out alive.

He got rapid response from the policemen as soon as they realized that he was not a commoner. They contacted his family members and told them to go ahead to the university teaching hospital to await their arrival. He would have preferred to be flown abroad if he had a choice but life was ebbing out of him.

I was there when they brought him to an available consulting area. His voice rang out loud in my ears as the several doctors and relatives milled round him. The police had finished their bit and were no longer visible in the ward. His relatives tried to encourage him while his wife cried profusely. His brothers, sisters and friends were there but none of his children was there. These people were like pests to the doctors.

One of his siblings who was very vocal in asking for prompt medical attention for his brother was given the prescription sheet to quickly procure drugs. The man and others with him apparently didn't have money evident by the fact that that they started passing the prescription sheet one to another. The Doctor bellowed at them to hurry to get the drugs as it was an emergency. Two or three of them left at that point maybe to source for money for the drugs. The vocal brother was very quiet.

Some others were asked to quickly go to the blood bank to donate blood for their brother. Surprisingly, none of them was willing to donate blood. They started debating and asking who could donate. One said he just recovered from an illness. Two or more of them went to sort that out.

The crying wife had been led out by friends and relatives. She didn't have access to her husband anymore.

The dying man who had been quiet for a while started pleading in a loud voice saying "Doctor, don't let me die; please doctor, don't let me die." The doctors assured him he wasn't going to die.

I observed the attitude of the doctors and knew that they had given up on the man. They knew he wasn't going to make it and they were just waiting for the moment. I learnt that the buying of drugs and blood was a regular gimmick to put the noisy relatives out so that they could concentrate on whatever needed to be done.

At that point in time when he needed God most, his hopes were on human doctors. I think he should have kept on saying 'God help me' instead of crying to the doctor not to let him die. He died shortly after - not a single relative was around. He was covered up and the bed area sealed off while the security kept the family out of the area. I was there and watched as he gave up the ghost.

I recalled when he was brought in struggling to cover his nakedness. He wore no pants and his pair of trousers was badly torn while his voice was audible. With time, his hand drooped and his voice started dying off. I didn't know he was gone until they pulled a sheet over him.

I think God was generous to him. He gave him more than twenty four hours to repent of his sins and prepare to meet his maker. I hope he made good use of that time. Many people don't have such a privilege to ruminate over their life and be able to come to terms that they might soon be standing before the judgment throne. Bible says it is appointed unto man once to die and then comes judgment. This is an appointment every man has to keep.

His work was finished. Business was finished for him. It was all over. His wife couldn't hear his last word and no child was there. None of them was there! He was left alone with his maker who is *The Beginning and the End.*

I still remembered the red and black Yoruba *buba and sooro* (native attire) that he wore—maybe the *aso-ebi* (party uniform) for the occasion that he went.

What happened to the money in his briefcase?

Were the drugs prescribed actually needed?

God fulfilled His part. He was not torn to shreds by animals. He didn't decay before he was found. At least he would be given a befitting burial.

The man's driver had his regrets. Why did he leave his master when he needed him most? Who would he now be driving? What would happen to all the man's plans and promises?

I recalled some Bible Passages:

When a man dies, all his plans die with him.
In that day, all his purposes come to an end.
All his plans are gone
His plans come to an end
His plans evaporate
His plans are bound to fail.
His plans come to nothing.
Don't put your confidence in a man to help you.
He can drop dead any time.

Psalm 146:1 – 4

For the living know that they shall die: but the dead
know not anything, neither have they any more a
reward; for the memory of them is forgotten.

Eccl 9:5

We should give thanks to God in all things. The man was privileged to have moments with God to make things right. God was aware of his location and made a way where there seemed to be no way.

15

The Sinister Niece

I had an office next to a crèche and sometimes the manager of the crèche, an elderly lady would invite me to pray for the children there. On a particular day, she informed me that she had a challenge. One of her clients brought her niece who had come from the village to visit her. She was barely ten years old. The client didn't feel comfortable leaving her baby at home with the niece hence she brought both of them to the crèche. She pleaded for ancillary services to teach her niece basic Arithmetic and English which she was ready to pay for.

However, the crèche manager observed that the niece often slept off with her legs on the wall and suspected some foul play. It is a traditional belief that witches travel into the realm of the spirit by raising their legs up on the wall. The

Manager was worried about the spiritual safety of babies in her custody.

The girl looked very harmless to me but after the prayers, she was singing like a jail-bird. She pleaded with me in a mature way that she wanted to confess her activities in the spirit realm.

I was stunned as she reeled out her nefarious activities.

She had friends with whom she went for meetings in the depths of some river. She was given a candy by a girl in the village but the girl and her friends came diabolically at night to force her to attend their meeting. When she expressed her unwillingness to follow them they explained that she had eaten their candy which had initiated her into their group and she was to follow them henceforth to their meetings. She could not resist them and though her body was in the house, her spirit went with them. She narrated how they did that constantly in the night and sometimes during daytime – the reason she habitually slept in the crèche at noon. They usually walked through grave yards before getting to their river destination she said.

She narrated her ordeals on some of these journeys. There was an occasion when they gave a three year old boy some candy but the boy refused to follow them at night. They however dragged him along. When they got to some graveyard and could no longer cope with him, they handed him over to some grave spirits. The spirits rejoiced; the boy screamed for help while they continued their journey. I interjected if she knew what the fate of the boy was. She responded that the boy died in his sleep at home. His parents discovered that in the morning.

She continued her horrific tale that they would remove their clothes and walk into the river where several others were gathered. The meetings were like celebrations and there were very many people. The meetings continued late into the nights and they were exhausted by the time they returned home in the early hours of the morning. Hardly was there a day they didn't go for these meetings.

Some of the things she told me were just incomprehensible. I asked why she was telling me all these. She said that she didn't want to follow them anymore because they did wicked things to people. She further explained that they were rewarded for bringing new people into their kingdom and probably sanctioned for not doing so. Also, she loved school but the night meetings always left her too exhausted to stay awake to learn.

Her aunt was too shocked to believe the strange stories she repeated. We asked if she had initiated her only baby and she replied in the negative. I will spare you the details of what transpired but she was returned to her people in the village.

The devil has let down several nets to capture as many people as he can. I wonder what had happened to many babies and children that had died in their sleep. It is written in the Bible that the enemies are busy sowing tares in the farm while the farm owner sleeps. The devil is luring and strategically targeting children and youths with the mandate to ruin their lives while their parents are busy pursuing position, power and affluence.

I recently watched a documentary on Africa war zones which showed how children soldiers were recruited and trained as mercenaries to kill, steal and destroy – they were brutal and ruthless. Some of them were too small for the weight of the guns they carried. Their parents were killed before their very eyes and forced to ravage other communities.

There could be danger at our doorsteps if we choose to be ignorant of the happenings in the spirit realm. According to the Bible, there is warfare against demonic forces, rulers of the darkness of the world, spiritual wickedness in high places amongst others. People who are in Christ are impervious to such attacks but ignorant people fall headlong into satanic traps sooner or later and place their children at risk.

There are two Managers in the spirit realm. One is rough, a taskmaster, a slave driver and a pseudo manager; the other is kind and gentle, protective and loving. It would soon be a matter of choice.

> *If it had not been the LORD who was on our side, when men rose up against us: Then they had swallowed us up quick, when their wrath was kindled against us: Then the waters had overwhelmed us, the stream had gone over our soul: Then the proud waters had gone over our soul. Blessed be the LORD, who hath not given us as a prey to their teeth. Our soul is escaped as a bird out of the snare of the fowlers: the snare is broken, and we are escaped.*
> *Our help is in the name of the LORD, who made heaven and earth.*
>
> *Psalms 124:2-8*

Conclusion

I find the Bible story in the tenth chapter of *Acts of the Apostles* very intriguing

An angel appeared to Cornelius and gave him some instructions to invite Simon Peter to his home in Caesarea. The angel told him Peter's name and surname as well as described vividly where he had taken up temporary residence as a guest of one Simon. The angel also knew the occupation of Peter's host – a tanner. He gave a perfect description of his house which was by the sea shore in Joppa.

Furthermore, the angel also went ahead of Cornelius' team to Joppa to inform Peter in his dream that he was going to have some strange guests whom he was to go with.

This story got me thinking deeply. God indeed exists and knows everything about us. He can always find us no matter how fast we think we can run. I concluded that it was wise to seek God who is the manufacturer of our life.

I realized that I was a bad manager of my life and needed to come under a new management. I therefore chose Jesus having identified Him as an effective and efficient manager. I also stopped running from Him and decided to walk towards him. I dared to call Him Lord and prayed to Him to reveal Himself to me. I also sincerely asked Jesus to please forgive all my sins.

I challenge you to sincerely pray to have this new Manager and you will be surprised that the one who created eyes and ears can indeed see and hear you. Come! Taste and see that the Lord is good.